First edition 2012

Library of Congress Cataloging-in-Publication Data is available.
Library of Congress Catalog Card Number pending
ISBN 978-0-7636-5896-0

12 13 14 15 16 17 SCP 10 9 8 7 6 5 4 3 2 1

Printed in Humen, Dongguan, China

This book was typeset in Cochin.
The illustrations were done in ink and watercolor.

Candlewick Press
99 Dover Street
Somerville, Massachusetts 02144

visit us at www.candlewick.com

THE ADVENTURES OF
LITTLE NUTBROWN HARE

Sam McBratney

CANDLEWICK PRESS

The Hiding Tree

Little Nutbrown Hare woke up one
morning and could hardly believe his eyes.
His favorite tree, the Hiding Tree,
was lying on the ground.

He called it the Hiding Tree
because it was hollow inside and
you could easily hide in there.
Not anymore, though. There had
been a storm in the night.

Big Nutbrown Hare scrambled up through
the roots and stood on the trunk of the tree.

That is a long way up, thought
Little Nutbrown Hare.

With a hop and a skip, Big Nutbrown Hare
went to the other end and peeped
through the leaves.

"Are you coming?"

"No, it's too high,"
said Little Nutbrown Hare—
and off he went to look
for interesting things
on the ground.

In the afternoon he played hide-and-seek with Big Nutbrown Hare. When it was his turn to hide, he came once more to where his favorite tree, the Hiding Tree, was lying on its side.

That would be the best hiding place ever!

Up through the roots he scrambled. I could go over and hide in the leaves, he thought.

Big Nutbrown Hare was counting. In a moment he would sing out, "Here I come, ready or not!"

With some careful hops . . . then a bit of a wobble . . .
and one last good jump . . .

Little Nutbrown Hare went along
the trunk of the tree to hide among
the branches and the leaves.

Now it was important to be absolutely still.

Big Nutbrown Hare looked here
and there . . .

and everywhere—

or so he thought.

"I give up,"
he shouted at last.
"You must have the best
hiding place ever!"

Little Nutbrown Hare
came tumbling down from
the Hiding Tree.

Big Nutbrown Hare was amazed.

"But I thought you were afraid to go up there!"

"I'm not afraid anymore," said
Little Nutbrown Hare,
laughing.

On Cloudy Mountain

Little Nutbrown Hare and
Big Nutbrown Hare set out one morning
to climb Cloudy Mountain. They liked to
be up high and look down at the fields, and
some of the plants that grew on
Cloudy Mountain were very tasty.

After lunch, Little Nutbrown Hare
played in the waterfalls among the rocks.
And then—better still—he found some
dandelions just ready for blowing.

One . . . two . . . three . . . *whooo*.

Half of a seed head was gone.

"That's good blowing,"
said Big Nutbrown Hare.

One . . . two . . . three . . . *whooo*.

Little Nutbrown Hare did an even better blow.

Away went the dandelion seeds,

almost every one.

And there were so many more,

all ready to be blown!

Big Nutbrown Hare had noticed something,
however. The clouds were coming farther
and farther down the mountain.
Soon they wouldn't be able to see a thing.

"We have to go home now," he said.

"I'm still blowing!" said Little Nutbrown Hare.

"I know," said Big Nutbrown Hare.
"But the clouds are coming
and we have to go."

You're spoiling all my fun,
Little Nutbrown Hare
was thinking.

But the mist was
getting thicker
every moment.

Which way was up

and which was down?

All of a sudden Big Nutbrown Hare
was right there beside him.

"Come with me now," he said.

Together they ran
down the mountain,
out of the clouds, and
into the sunny day below.

"Well, *that* certainly was an adventure!"
said Big Nutbrown Hare. "I'm sorry
I had to stop your fun like that."

"You nearly got lost!"
said Little Nutbrown Hare.

"Nearly," smiled Big Nutbrown Hare,
glancing up once more at
Cloudy Mountain.
"But what matters is—
I found you."

The Far Field

Early one morning Little Nutbrown Hare
ran all the way to the Far Field.
He called it the Far Field because it was farther
than the Hiding Tree, over the river,
and beyond Cloudy Mountain.

He discovered an interesting hole beneath
the trees and wondered what was in there.

"Come away," said a voice. "It's best
not to bother with holes in the ground."

It was Big Nutbrown Hare watching over him.

So Little Nutbrown Hare came away
from the hole and jumped over
some toadstools instead.

There was a pond nearby. The leaves of the water plants looked like stepping-stones across the water.

"No, no," said a voice.
"That water might be deep. Come away."

It was Big Nutbrown Hare
telling him to be careful.

So Little Nutbrown Hare skipped away from
the pond and found another place to play.

Then, in the thickness of the meadow grass,
he discovered a bird's nest. Four speckled
eggs lay there, lovely and smooth.

"Come away," someone whispered.
"Birds don't like anyone near their nests."
Once again Big Nutbrown Hare was close by.

Together they hopped away from the nest with its
precious eggs, to search the meadow grass
for juicy plants to eat.

Later that day, Little Nutbrown Hare went
back to the interesting hole beneath the trees.
Still he couldn't see a thing in there,
which made him wonder all the more.

What would be down a hole like that?

He looked around and saw no one else.
He was all alone.

I think I might go down there,
thought Little Nutbrown Hare. . . .

Then a voice said, "No.
Dark holes are dangerous."

This time it was his own little voice
inside his head, and it was
telling him to be careful.

So Little Nutbrown Hare came away from
the hole and chased some daddy longlegs
through the Far Field instead.

Coming Home

Little Nutbrown Hare and Big Nutbrown Hare were wandering home at the end of the day.

"Can you guess the place I like best in the whole world?" said Little Nutbrown Hare, who loved to play games.

"Your favorite place?" asked Big Nutbrown Hare.

"Yes. In the world."

Big Nutbrown Hare began to think.
He knew that Little Nutbrown Hare
liked lots of places, but which one
did he like best?

"Is it . . . Cloudy Mountain?"

"No, that's too high up."

On they went, hopping home together.
Big Nutbrown Hare was thinking so hard
that he didn't see where he was going.

"Wet feet!" he said. "Ah,
is your favorite place . . .
the river?"

"No," Little Nutbrown Hare said, laughing.
"That's too wet."

On they went hopping home, until

Big Nutbrown Hare suddenly stopped.

He'd just had a good idea.

"Is your favorite place *across* the river?
Could it be . . . the Far Field?"

"No, that's too far away."

On they ran quite quickly now, for the sun was sinking fast. Then Big Nutbrown Hare spotted something that made him think.

"Do we play games in this place
you're thinking of? Could it be . . .
the Hiding Tree?"

"No. But my favorite place has some leaves."

Goodness me! thought Big Nutbrown Hare.
Not Cloudy Mountain. Not the river.
Not the Far Field. Some leaves,
but not the Hiding Tree.

"Well . . . I think you'll
have to tell me,"
he said at last.

"We're here! *Home* is my best place of all."

"Well, of course!"
said Big Nutbrown Hare.
"I should have guessed!"

The early stars were shining already.

Big Nutbrown Hare settled
Little Nutbrown Hare into his bed of leaves,
where soon he closed his eyes.

"And where *you* are," whispered
Big Nutbrown Hare, "is the best place
in the whole world for me."